# THE BEAR

## FAIR

## by Stan and

GROLIER BOOK CLUB EDITION

BEGINNER BOOKS
A Division of Random House, Inc.

# DETECTIVES

## THE CASE OF THE MISSING PUMPKIN.

# Jan Berenstain

Copyright © 1975 by Stanley and Janice Berenstain. All rights reserved under International and Pan-American Copyright Conventions. Published in the United States by Random House, Inc., New York, and simultaneously in Canada by Random House of Canada Limited, Toronto. Library of Congress Cataloging in Publication Data. Berenstain, Stanley. The Bear detectives and the case of the prize pumpkin. "B-60." SUMMARY: The Bear family don their detective gear and try to solve the mystery of the missing prize pumpkin. [1. Bears—Fiction. 2. Stories in rhyme] I. Berenstain, Janice, joint author. II. Title. PZ8.3.B4493Bf [E] 75-1603 ISBN 0-394-83127-6 ISBN 0-394-93127-0 lib. bdg. Manufactured in the United States of America.

The Spooky Stranger

Who can it be?

Papa Bear
and Snuff

Will they
be much help?

Will the Bear Detectives get their bear?

Help!
My pumpkin won
first prize at the fair.
Now I can't find it
anywhere!

FAIR

THE
BEAR
DETECTIVES

Do not worry,
Farmer Ben.
The BEAR DETECTIVES
will find it again!

THE
BEAR
DETECTIVES

Your prize pumpkin stolen?
Never fear.
Great Bear Detective Pop is here!
I will find it.
You will see.

Just watch
my old dog Snuff and me.

But, Papa,
our Bear Detective Book
will tell us how
to catch the crook.

"Lesson One.
First look around
for any TRACKS
that are on the ground."

Don't waste your time
with books and stuff!
We're on the trail!
Just follow Snuff!

We'll catch that crook.
We'll show you how.
Snuff and I
will catch the . . .

. . . cow?

MooOO

Say! Look down there!
Do you see what I see?

There's a
**WHEELBARROW TRACK**
going by this tree!

A good detective
writes things down:

"Checked out a cow,
white and brown."

The track ends here.
What shall we do?

We'll look in the book.

It says,
"Lesson Two.
Look all around
for another clue."

Humf! You can look around
as much as you please.
I'm going to follow
these carrots and peas . . .

. . . and eggshells
and corncobs
and other stuff.

This must be the way!
Let's go, Snuff!

MUNCH MUNCH CRUNCH GOBBLE

Listen, Snuff!
Hear that munching?
That pumpkin thief is
pumpkin lunching!

O.K., thief!
You've munched your last.
Your pumpkin-stealing
days are past.

Look here! Look here,
Papa Bear.
We found a new clue
over there.

You see
we found
a PUMPKIN LEAF . . .

Aha!
You've found a pumpkin leaf.
Just show me where
you found this leaf.
Then <u>I</u> will find that
pumpkin thief.

The pumpkin thief!
I've found him, Snuff!
Let's grab him quick.
He sure looks tough.

Be careful, Pop.
Lesson Three in the book
says, "Before you leap,
be sure to look."

Hang on, Snuff!
Hold him tight!
This pumpkin thief
can really fight.

Did you find any clues
in that scarecrow, Pop?
Shall we keep on looking,
or shall we stop?

Hmmmmmmmmm . . .
Checked out a cow,
three pigs in a pen,
and a scarecrow owned
by Farmer Ben.

Found some tracks
and a pumpkin leaf.
Still haven't found
that pumpkin thief.

Look! By that haystack!
I see something blue!
It's the first-prize ribbon.
That's a very good clue!

A haystack!
The perfect place
to hide.

I'll bet the thief
is right inside.

Pumpkin thief,
don't try to run.
Your pumpkin-stealing
days are done!

But, Papa . . .

I was trying to say,
I don't think the thief
is in THAT hay.

Hmmmmmm . . .
Ben's haystack
is another spot
where the pumpkin thief
is not.

Say! Look over there!
Look in that door!
PUMPKIN SEEDS
all over the floor!

He's in the barn! This is it!
Hand me that detective kit.

I'll snap on these handcuffs.
I'll take him to jail.
Pumpkin thief,
it's the end of the trail.

Old Snuff,
this may be tough.

It looks
like we've caught
a whole GANG
of crooks.

Hmmmmm . . .
Checked out a cow,
brown and white.
Checked out a scarecrow
after a fight.

Checked out a haystack.
Three pigs in a pen . . .
Put the cuffs on
Farmer Ben's hen.

Found some tracks,
a ribbon, a leaf . . .
some pumpkin seeds,

BUT STILL
NO THIEF!

Small Bear, I guess you better look
at what it says there in your book.

Lesson Four—
here's how it goes—
"A good detective
will USE HIS NOSE!"

Hmmmmmmm . . .
Pumpkin seeds,
pumpkin shell—
and . . .
aha!
I smell a
PUMPKIN SMELL!

The pumpkin was pied
by Mrs. Ben.

The case is solved.
Good work, men!
The BEAR DETECTIVES
have done it again!

MMMMMMM!
My dear, you and I
will SHARE first prize.
ME for the pumpkin,
YOU for the pies!

# Stan and Jan Berenstain

For years Stan and Jan Berenstain were well-known to millions of adult readers for their many marvelously funny books and magazine features on family life in America. Then, with THE BIG HONEY HUNT, children discovered that they also wrote marvelously funny books about family life in Bear Country. Since then millions of beginning readers have enjoyed the misadventures of the famous Bear Family.

The Berenstains went to the same art school (the Philadelphia Museum School), enjoy the same food, tastes and hobbies, have the same two sons, and as far as can be discovered, type simultaneously on the same typewriter and draw simultaneously on the same piece of paper. They work together in the same studio in Elkins Park, Pennsylvania, creating words and pictures that delight bears and children around the world.